South Downs

river

Ben's house

Button found here

Sky found here

Chicken coop

Farmyard

Calf barn

Jasmine's house

Holly found here

Lucky born here

Jasmine Green Rescues
A Lamb
Called Lucky

Read all the books in the
Jasmine Green Rescues series

Jasmine Green Rescues
A Lamb Called Lucky

Helen Peters
illustrated by Ellie Snowdon

WALKER BOOKS

Text copyright © 2018 by Helen Peters
Illustrations copyright © 2018 by Ellie Snowdon

First US edition 2021
First published by Nosy Crow (UK) 2018

Library of Congress Catalog Card Number pending
ISBN 978-1-5362-1028-6 (hardcover)
ISBN 978-1-5362-1604-2 (paperback)

20 21 22 23 24 25 LBM 10 9 8 7 6 5 4 3 2 1

Printed in Melrose Park, IL, USA

This book was typeset in Bembo.
The illustrations were done in pencil with a digital wash overlay.

Walker Books US
a division of
Candlewick Press
99 Dover Street
Somerville, Massachusetts 02144

www.walkerbooksus.com

For Rosie and Jack
HP

For Papa
ES

1
Like Baby Dinosaurs

"We have to go in for lunch now, Truffle," said Jasmine, scratching her pet pig behind the ears. "We'll come and see you again this afternoon."

The huge sow gave a contented grunt and lay down under an apple tree. It was hard to believe it now, but Truffle had been a tiny little runt when Jasmine had found her. Jasmine and her best friend, Tom, were planning to run an animal rescue center when they grew up, and Truffle had been their first rescue animal.

In the farmhouse mudroom, Jasmine's cats, Toffee and Marmite, lay curled up in their bed on the work surface. Her collie, Sky, was sleeping on his bed on the floor.

"Look at him," said Jasmine. "That training session tired him out."

Jasmine had found Sky last summer, abandoned and starving. He was a year old now, and Jasmine was training him as a sheepdog.

"We'll be able to give him lots of training now that it's vacation," said Tom.

"Is that you, Jas?" called her mom from the kitchen. "Wash your hands and come in for lunch."

"Coming," called Jasmine.

The rest of her family was already sitting around the kitchen table. Sixteen-year-old Ella had a book propped open in front of her, as usual. Manu, who was six, was wriggling in his chair and chomping noisily on a sandwich, scattering crumbs all around him.

Jasmine handed Tom a bread roll and took one herself. She reached across the table for the cheese.

"Is there any dessert?" asked Manu.

"There's fruit in the bowl," said Mom.

"Didn't you do baking at school yesterday?" asked Dad. "I thought you said you were making cookies."

"That's right, you did," said Mom. "As an Easter present for your family. Are they still in your book bag?"

Manu looked sheepish. "Oh, yes," he said. "I'll get them."

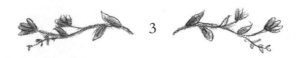

He walked over to the pegs on the wall. From his book bag, he produced a clear plastic box. It contained one small cookie.

"Is that it?" asked Dad. "You made one cookie?"

"Yes," said Manu, studiously avoiding all eye contact.

"Really?" said Mom. "You spent all afternoon making one cookie?"

"Yes."

Everyone's eyes were fixed on Manu as he looked down at the table. After a few seconds, he glanced up at his family. Then he looked down again.

"I might have made more than one," he said.

"Oh?" said Dad. "What happened to the others?"

"They fell on the floor."

"Really?"

"Yes."

"Really?" said Dad. "Would that have been the floor of your stomach?"

Mom tried not to laugh. "I guess you've already

4

had your dessert, then," she said. "Have some fruit if you're still hungry."

"Should Tom and I check the sheep after lunch?" asked Jasmine.

"That would be great," said Dad. "Then Mom and I can get on with the tuberculosis testing."

Jasmine's dad was a farmer and her mom was a vet. That afternoon they were going to be testing the cows for TB. All the cows had to be tested every year to stop the disease from spreading.

"Ben's mom is picking you up at two o'clock," Mom said to Manu. "Ella, can you make sure he's ready, please?"

Ella, deep in her book, didn't respond. Mom repeated the request.

"What?" said Ella vaguely.

Mom sighed. "Manu, go and get your swimming things now, will you? Then you'll be ready to go when Ben gets here."

Ben was Manu's best friend. Like Tom, he spent as much time at the farm as he could, but because

Mom and Dad were working this afternoon, Ben's mom was taking them both swimming.

Dad was reading an article in *Farmers Weekly*. "There's a lot of sheep rustling going on at the moment," he said. "This poor farmer in Yorkshire had his whole flock taken."

"How can anyone steal a whole flock of sheep?" asked Manu.

"Well-trained dogs and a big truck," said Dad.

"Will they take our sheep?"

Dad shook his head. "This is all hundreds of miles away."

"Come on, Tom," said Jasmine, stuffing the last of her roll into her mouth. "Let's go and see the lambs."

Lambing season was Jasmine's favorite time of year at Oak Tree Farm, and the lambing barn was her favorite place. And now, she thought happily, she had two whole weeks with no school and new lambs being born every day.

They could hear the lambs long before they saw them. Their high-pitched bleats and their mothers' low answering calls could be heard all across the farmyard. To a stranger, they might all sound the same. But every one of those lambs could recognize its mother's call among the baa-ing of a hundred other ewes, and every ewe could tell the cry of her own lamb.

The big barn was divided into pens with metal rails. Along the left-hand side were rows of small pens, each containing a single ewe and her lambs. Most of these had only been born yesterday. In the largest pen were the sheep with older lambs. They would be taken out to the field in a few days' time.

Jasmine scanned the animals for any signs of trouble. Sometimes a lamb that had seemed perfectly healthy would suddenly die for no apparent reason. But they all looked well this afternoon.

She turned her attention to the most exciting pen of all, where the sheep still waiting to lamb

were kept. A smile spread across her face as she saw a ewe standing in the middle of the pen with two tiny newborn lambs sucking vigorously from her udder, wiggling their little tails as they fed.

"Look," she said to Tom. "Aren't they gorgeous?"

It never ceased to amaze Jasmine that newborn lambs somehow always knew exactly what they

8

needed to do. Just a few minutes after they were born, they would heave themselves up on their wobbly legs, stagger to their mother's udder, and start to drink.

Unless there was something wrong, of course. That was why somebody had to check the sheep every few hours. But there was nothing wrong with these two.

Jasmine and Tom scattered fresh straw on the floor and filled up the hay racks and water buckets. When they were finished, Tom said, "Should we go and give Sky another training session?"

They were about to leave the barn when Jasmine glimpsed something bright yellow lying in the straw. She bent down to examine it and drew in her breath.

"What is it?" asked Tom. He crouched beside her.

"Oh!" he gasped.

The flash of yellow that Jasmine had seen was the edge of a beak. It belonged to a tiny baby bird, sprawled in the straw. And now Jasmine saw another identical baby bird, nearly buried in the straw beside it.

They must have been almost newly hatched, because their eyes were closed and they had no feathers at all, just shiny skin, pink with patches of scaly gray on the wings and head, and a gray line down the back.

You couldn't really call them cute. In fact, they were remarkably ugly. They looked more like baby dinosaurs than birds.

"They must have fallen out of the nest," said Tom. "I can't believe they're still alive."

They watched the birds' tiny chests rise and fall with their heartbeats.

"They won't survive much longer on their own," said Jasmine. "We have to do something to help them."

2
The Right Thing to Do

"We need to put them back in their nest," said Tom.

They stepped back and scanned the big metal beams that held up the barn roof. Where the beams crisscrossed each other, there were plenty of nooks and crannies where a bird could have built a nest.

Careful not to step on the baby birds, Jasmine walked a few paces forward to look from the other side.

"I can't see a nest," said Tom.

"Me neither," said Jasmine. "And we couldn't put them back up there anyway. Those beams are way too high, even for Dad's massive ladder."

"Anyway, their parents might have rejected them on purpose," said Tom, "so if we put them back, they might push them out again."

"Or there might be more than one nest up there," said Jasmine, "and then we wouldn't know which one to put them in. If we put them in the wrong one, the birds would push them out. And they might not survive another fall."

"So," said Tom, looking excited, "I guess we're going to have to look after them ourselves."

Jasmine grinned at him. "I guess we are."

"Do you know what they eat?"

"No, but we can look it up. Mom would know, but we can't ask her while she's TB testing, and she won't be finished for hours."

"Come on, then," said Tom. "Let's take them inside."

"I'll get something to put them in," said Jasmine, walking over to the pen where Dad kept the lambing supplies. She found an empty plastic tub and filled it with straw. Gently, she picked up the baby birds, laid them in the tub, and packed straw around them to keep them warm. Then she and Tom walked back to the house. It was very quiet, so Manu must have left for swimming. The house was never quiet when Manu was around.

They sat the tub on the kitchen table and Tom fetched Mom's laptop from her office. He typed "orphaned newborn bird" into the search engine and clicked on the website of a wildlife charity.

"Oh," he said. "That's not very helpful."

"What does it say?" asked Jasmine.

"It says they probably won't survive."

"Why not?"

"It says rearing a baby bird is time-consuming and difficult, and the chance of success is very low. It says you should only attempt it as a last

resort, and you should really take it to an expert rehabilitator."

"I bet that's what Mom will say," said Jasmine. "Like when she wanted us to take Button to the wildlife rehabilitator. It's lucky she's not here."

Last spring, Jasmine and Tom had rescued a clutch of duck eggs from the riverbank, after the mother duck was killed by a dog. Button had hatched from one of the eggs, and now he was a handsome drake who lived with the free-range chickens.

"What about when she comes back, though?" asked Tom. "She might make us take them to a rehabilitator."

"We'll just have to prove we can look after them ourselves," said Jasmine. "If we learn what to do, and we do everything it says, I don't see how we'd be any different from a professional."

The first thing to do, they discovered, was to keep the birds warm in a nest made from a bowl lined

with tissues, placed on top of a hot water bottle.

Tom filled the kettle and switched it on, while Jasmine lined a small plastic bowl with tissues. When the kettle boiled, Tom filled the hot water bottle and they sat the baby birds in their new nest on top of it.

"It says you should put the nest in a quiet, dark place where it won't be disturbed," said Tom.

"Nowhere that Manu can get to it, then," said Jasmine.

"What about your wardrobe?" Tom suggested.

"Yes, that might work. I'll have to be really careful to keep the bedroom door closed, though, so the cats can't get in."

"It's only for a couple of weeks," said Tom, looking at the website. "Once they start to hop around, you're supposed to put them in a cage and leave it outdoors during the daytime, so they can get used to the outside world."

One of the birds stretched its head and neck up high and started to chirp. Its beak opened so wide that it looked as though its head would split in two.

"Wow," said Tom, as the other bird started to chirp, too. "They're really hungry."

"What does it say we should give them to eat?" asked Jasmine.

Tom scrolled down the page. "Canned cat food mashed up with water."

"Oh, good, that's easy. It's lucky we have cats."

"You have to use tweezers to drop tiny pieces into the back of their mouths," said Tom, "and wipe the beak clean with cotton balls afterward."

"I'll get the tweezers and cotton balls," said Jasmine, "and you mash up the cat food."

When she came back, Tom had mashed cat food and water into a revolting-looking brown paste. "You're supposed to feed them pieces about half the size of your little fingernail," he said.

Jasmine looked at her little fingernail. "That's tiny. Do you want to feed them?"

"We can take turns," said Tom. "You go first."

Jasmine picked up a little piece of food with the tweezers. She held the tweezers over the first gaping beak and dropped the food in.

The tiny creature gulped it down. Jasmine did the same with the other bird. It was very satisfying to see them eat.

She passed the tweezers to Tom. "How much do we feed them?" she asked.

"It says they just stop when they're full," said Tom. "They only eat a little at a time, but you have to feed them every half hour."

"Every half hour! At night, too?"

18

"No, just in the daytime."

"Phew." Jasmine didn't mind the idea of getting up in the middle of the night, but twice every hour did seem like a bit much.

After a few mouthfuls, the birds closed their beaks. Jasmine wiped them clean. Then she looked at her watch to see when they would need their next feeding.

"Lucky it's vacation," she said, "or we'd never be able to do it."

"I wonder what type of bird they are," said Tom. He searched online for a chart to identify baby birds, but so many of the babies looked alike that it was impossible to tell for certain.

"We'll have to wait until they get feathers," said Jasmine.

"What should we call them?" asked Tom.

Jasmine thought for a minute. "This one can be Peanut," she said. "That's a good name for a bird."

"Peanut," said Tom thoughtfully. "And the other one can be Popcorn."

"Peanut and Popcorn," said Jasmine. "Perfect."

"It says you can mark them with a little dab of food coloring on the top of their heads, to tell them apart," said Tom.

"Oh, that will be so cute."

"I bet they'll miss their parents," Tom said.

"We'll have to pet them a lot," said Jasmine, "to make up for it."

"Do you want to keep them as pets?" asked Tom.

Jasmine shook her head. "No. I hate seeing birds in cages. I want to release them when they're ready."

"Then you can't pet them." Tom scrolled up the page. "It says if we pet them, or even talk to them, they'll imprint on us, and then they won't ever be able to live in the wild."

Jasmine knew about imprinting. Baby birds became attached to the first thing they saw and thought it was their mother. Button had imprinted on Jasmine, and she had loved having a duckling as a companion. But ducks were different, and Button lived happily in the farmyard with the chickens now. If Peanut and Popcorn became attached to her, they would never be able to live in the wild with other birds. They would have to be pets forever.

She looked at the tiny creatures in their nest of tissues. Jasmine loved having pets, and she was constantly trying to persuade her parents to take on more animals. But it felt so wrong that

creatures who were born to fly freely should be kept in a space where all they could do was hop from perch to perch.

"I want them to be able to live in the wild," she said. "So we can't talk to them or pet them."

"That's going to be so hard," said Tom.

"I know. But it's the right thing to do."

3
Are You Up to Something?

Much later that afternoon, the back door rattled open. Tom had just finished feeding Popcorn and Peanut for the eighth time.

"Jasmine, Tom!" It was Mom's voice. "Are you up there?"

"Quick," said Jasmine. "Put them in the wardrobe."

Tom placed the nest in the bottom of the wardrobe and closed the door. Jasmine pushed the food bowl, tweezers, and cotton balls under her bed just as Mom appeared in the doorway, a pile of folded laundry in her arms.

"Sorry that took so long," she said. "You must be starving."

Jasmine's attention had been so focused on the chicks that she had forgotten about dinner, but now she realized she was really hungry.

"I thought you might like to go out for pizza," said Mom, "since it's the first day of vacation. And also because I haven't gone grocery shopping."

Jasmine's mouth watered at the thought of her favorite food. Pizza was Tom's favorite, too. But she knew he was thinking the same thing as she was. They caught each other's eyes anxiously.

"Er . . . actually, can we stay in?" she asked. "We can just have beans on toast or something. We're not that hungry."

Mom stared at her. "But you love going out for pizza. I thought you'd be really excited."

"I know. Sorry. Thank you. It's just . . . We're

kind of in the middle of something. Making something."

Mom scanned the floor. "I don't see anything. What are you making?"

Jasmine could have kicked herself. Why had she said they were making something?

"I mean, making up something. Poems. It's our vacation homework, to write a poem."

At least that part was true, she thought. They did have to write a poem.

Mom looked surprised and slightly confused. "Well, if you're really happy with beans on toast, I should be able to manage that."

"Yes please," said Jasmine. "Thank you, Mom."

"Thank you," said Tom.

"I'll just put these clothes away," said Mom.

She walked over to the wardrobe. Jasmine and Tom leaped up.

"We'll do it," said Jasmine, snatching the clothes from her mother.

Mom looked at her suspiciously. "What's going on?"

"Nothing. We're just trying to help. You must be tired after all that TB testing."

Mom didn't look convinced. "Are you up to something, Jasmine?"

"Of course not," said Jasmine with her most wide-eyed, innocent look. "We're just in the middle of planning our poems, that's all."

With a last thoughtful look at Jasmine, Mom left the room.

"Phew," said Jasmine. "That was close."

"This is going to be hard," said Tom. "We need to walk Sky, too."

"One of us will have to walk him while the other one looks after the birds. Will you be able to come up every day?"

"Of course," said Tom, "if I don't leave Holly for too long."

Holly was Tom's cat, and they were devoted to each other.

"Do you think we should tell your mom?" asked Tom. "You know, because of what those websites say about orphaned baby birds not surviving."

"But if we tell her," Jasmine said, "she'll just take them to a rehabilitator. And I don't believe they could look after them any better than we could. We're doing everything they say on the websites."

"Plus the rehabilitators are probably looking after tons of birds," said Tom. "We've only got Popcorn and Peanut, and there are two of us, so we can give them much more attention than they could."

"That's true," said Jasmine, impressed with his logic.

"And it won't be for long," said Tom. "Once they're about a week old, they start getting feathers, and then they only need feeding every forty-five minutes."

"We won't need to keep them secret for that long, anyway," said Jasmine. "If we tell Mom after a few days, she can't say we have to take them to a rehabilitator, because we'll have shown we can look after them ourselves."

"If they survive that long," said Tom.

"Of course they'll survive," said Jasmine. "We're going to make sure they do."

4
I'll Check the Sheep

The next morning Jasmine woke to a little cheeping sound coming from her wardrobe. She smiled as she realized what it was. Then fear gripped her stomach. What if that was only one bird cheeping?

She held her breath as she opened the wardrobe door.

Two huge beaks gaped up at her. Jasmine's shoulders dropped with relief.

"I'm coming, little ones," she whispered. "I'll just go and make you some food."

As she pulled on her clothes, she glanced at her alarm clock. She was pleased to see it was only a quarter to six. She liked being the first one up. It was so nice to have the house to herself for a while before anybody else was awake. Except for Dad, of course. He was always up early.

When she got downstairs, Dad was in the kitchen, speaking to somebody on the phone.

"Thanks for letting me know," he said. "I'll be there as soon as I can."

He put the phone down and turned to Jasmine. "Some guy in Foxdean woke up to find six calves in his back garden." He grabbed the keys to his truck from the top of the dresser. "Making a heck of a mess, apparently. I'm going to head over and round them up. What a nuisance."

"I can check the sheep for you," said Jasmine.

He looked at her gratefully. "Oh, thanks, Jas. I'd have asked Mom, but she's out on a call."

This was not unusual. When Mom was on call,

30

she often had to get up in the middle of the night for an animal emergency.

Dad took his coat off its peg. "I checked them at midnight," he said, "so with any luck everything will be fine." He went out to the mudroom, put his boots on, and unlocked the back door. "I'll be back as soon as I can."

"OK," said Jasmine. "Bye, Dad."

She followed him into the mudroom and took a packet of cat food from the cupboard. Sky got up from his bed and padded over to her, wagging his tail.

"Good morning, Sky," said Jasmine, stroking his soft coat. "I'm going to feed Popcorn and Peanut and check the sheep. Then I'll need to feed the chicks again, and after that I'll take you for a walk."

Toffee and Marmite were curled up in their bed. Jasmine opened the packet and squeezed most of the food into their dishes. Then she mashed up the rest in a bowl with some warm water.

31

She tiptoed back to her room. The cheeping was so loud that she was amazed it hadn't woken Ella and Manu. The baby birds were stretching their necks and heads as high as they could reach, their huge beaks gaping open. Jasmine had put a little dab of green food coloring on the top of Peanut's head last night, so she knew which bird was which.

When the chicks stopped feeding, Jasmine stored the rest of the food under her bed. Then she tiptoed back downstairs, put on her coat and boots, and walked across the yard to the lambing barn. Maybe there would be another set of twins, or even triplets.

She scanned the pen of

pregnant ewes. Her stomach gave a horrible lurch.

A ewe lay on her side in the straw. Her eyes were open, but she was frighteningly still. Beside her lay a shivering newborn lamb.

Jasmine hurried across the barn, knelt on the straw, and lifted the ewe's head.

It lay heavy in her hands. The open eyes were dull and her nose was dry. Jasmine could tell there was no life left in her.

The lamb was a boy, Jasmine saw. He lay trembling in the straw, still wet from his birth. His eyes were closed and his wrinkled coat was a yellowy color. When Jasmine touched him, he felt dangerously cold. She knew she didn't have much time to save him.

She rubbed him with a handful of straw to dry his damp wool and stimulate circulation. Then she grabbed an empty feed sack and filled it with fresh straw. She unzipped her coat, scooped the lamb into her arms, and wrapped her coat around him. Holding him tightly with one arm, she picked up the sack of straw with the other, climbed back over the gate, and hurried toward the farmhouse.

5
Poor Little Thing

Cradling the lamb under her coat, Jasmine grabbed an empty cardboard box from the garage and took it into the kitchen. She knelt on the tiled floor in front of the big Aga stove and laid the cold little lamb on her lap. His eyes were still closed and his breathing was fast and shallow. He looked very sick.

Jasmine half filled the box with straw and laid the lamb inside it. She lifted his head a little. When she took her hand away, it flopped back down in the straw. Her heart sank. If he couldn't hold up his own head, then he probably wouldn't be strong enough to swallow. It was vital to warm him up.

The Aga had four ovens, two on each side. The top right was the hottest and the bottom left was the coolest. It gave off a very gentle warmth, perfect for reviving sick baby animals.

"There you go, little one," said Jasmine, sliding the box into the oven and half closing the door. "That will warm you up. I'm going to make you some colostrum."

Colostrum was the mother's first milk. It contained a lot of protein, as well as vital antibodies to protect the newborn animal from disease. If the lamb's mother had died immediately after he was born, he would have had no colostrum. Jasmine could give him colostrum formula, but he had to be strong enough to swallow it.

From the cupboard under the mudroom sink, where Dad kept the supplies for bottle-fed lambs,

she fetched a plastic measuring jug, a tub of pow-
dered colostrum formula, a feeding bottle, and
a rubber teat. She read the instructions on the
tub, and then she measured the powder into the
jug, added the right amount of warm water, and
whisked the mixture until it was smooth. Then
she poured it into the bottle, screwed the teat on,
pushed up her sleeve, and squeezed a few drops
onto her wrist to check that it didn't feel either
hot or cold on the thin skin there.

It was a bit too warm, so she left it a minute and tested it again. This time, it felt just right. Carefully, she slid the cardboard box out of the oven.

"Come on, little lamb," Jasmine whispered, lifting him out of the box and arranging him in a sitting position on her lap. "If you drink your colostrum, you'll get better soon."

Even as she said this, she knew it wasn't necessarily true. Some lambs got better and some didn't. At this point, it was impossible to tell whether this one would revive or not.

Jasmine slipped her index finger inside his mouth and prized his jaws apart. She placed the teat in his mouth, hoping he would start to suck. But he didn't move.

The best way to give him colostrum would be through a stomach tube. But she couldn't do that herself, so she would have to teach him to suck from a teat.

She held the bottle in position with one hand while, with the other, she tried to move his jaw up and down to teach him to suck. It wasn't easy, and she couldn't tell whether he was actually getting any colostrum. The rich yellowy milk dribbled out the sides of his mouth. Was any of it going down his throat?

Jasmine looked at her watch. Oh, no! It was over half an hour since she had fed Popcorn and Peanut.

"Please drink, little lamb," she said. "I know it's not your fault, but I have two baby birds who need feeding, too."

She wished Tom were here to help. But seven o'clock was too early to phone him.

The mudroom door rattled open.

"Dad?" called Jasmine.

"It's me," came Mom's voice.

"Oh, I'm so glad you're back," said Jasmine as Mom appeared in the kitchen doorway. "Look. He's an orphan. I made him colostrum, but he can't suck. He needs it through a tube."

Mom went to the sink to wash her hands. "Where's Dad?" she asked.

"He had to go and round up some escaped calves at Foxdean. So I checked the sheep and there was a dead ewe with this poor little lamb beside her."

Mom looked at the lamb as she dried her hands. "He needs that colostrum quickly."

She went out to the mudroom and came back with a length of rubber tubing and a plastic syringe. She laid the tubing along the lamb's body from his mouth to his last rib. "That's where the stomach is. Make a mark on the tube with that pen, would you, so I know how far to insert it."

Jasmine made a mark on the tubing where it

40

lay next to the lamb's mouth. Then Mom ran the tube under the tap and inserted it. When Jasmine was younger, she worried that this would hurt the lamb, but they never seemed to mind. This one didn't make any fuss at all as the tube went down his throat.

Mom dipped the syringe into the bottle of colostrum and drew up the plunger. Then she attached the syringe to the tube and steadily pushed the plunger until all the colostrum had gone down the tube.

"There you are," she said to the lamb. "All fed. Pop him back in the Aga, Jas, and hopefully he'll start to improve soon."

She handed the lamb to Jasmine, who kissed the top of his head before she put him in his box.

"He feels warmer already," she said, sliding the box into the Aga. "It was lucky you came home."

"It's lucky you found him when you did," said Mom. "He wouldn't have survived much longer, poor little thing."

41

Suddenly, Jasmine smiled. "Lucky! That's what I'm going to call him."

"Don't get your hopes up too much," said Mom. "He's still got a long way to go."

Jasmine gave her mother a reproachful look. "He's going to be fine. I can tell."

"All right. Will you wash all the feeding things, please?" said Mom.

"In a minute," said Jasmine. "I just need to go upstairs."

Toffee was mewing and scratching at Jasmine's bedroom door, clearly desperate to get in. Jasmine shook her head at him.

"Oh, no, you don't," she said. "I know exactly what you want, and you're not getting anywhere near those baby birds."

She picked him up and set him down on the other side of the landing before she opened the door. But she had underestimated Toffee's speed. Before she had a chance to close the door behind

her, he had shot between her legs and across the room to the wardrobe, hooking his paw around the door to open it.

Jasmine ran to the wardrobe and grabbed Toffee around the middle. "No," she said in her strictest voice as she carried him out of the room. "I know it's your natural instinct and you don't understand about kindness to birds, but I'm looking after these chicks and I'm not letting you get near them."

She set Toffee down again on the landing and shut the door firmly in his face.

Popcorn and Peanut were cheeping desperately. Jasmine took the tweezers and food from under her bed and dropped little pieces into their gaping mouths until they closed their beaks.

She checked the time. She needed to take Sky out before breakfast. And with a lamb to look after as well, it wasn't going to be easy to sneak off every thirty minutes.

Maybe she should tell Mom about the birds

this morning, she thought. After all, she had kept them alive for long enough to prove she could look after them. If she told her about them now, surely Mom would let her care for them until they were old enough to be released.

6
A Few Shaky Steps

Jasmine brought Sky back to the house just as it was time to give Peanut and Popcorn their next feeding.

"Come and look at this, Jas," Mom called from the kitchen.

Jasmine opened the door and her face broke into an enormous smile. Lucky was sitting up in his box, looking out of the oven. When he saw Jasmine, he gave a little bleat and his hooves scrabbled around in the straw.

"He's revived!" cried Jasmine, running across the room. "He's trying to stand up! Oh, you clever little lamb." She knelt down and kissed his head. Lucky bleated again.

"You're talking, too! Oh, I'm so happy you're better."

"He's really perked up, hasn't he?" said Mom, who was cooking on the Aga. She picked up the frying pan and flipped a pancake.

"Ooh, pancakes!" said Jasmine.

"I thought you deserved your favorite breakfast, seeing as you've already saved a lamb's life this morning. Here, you can have the first one."

She slid the pancake onto a plate. Jasmine looked at it longingly. But she needed to walk Sky before she sat down to eat herself.

The door from the hall opened and Manu appeared in his pajamas, his hair sticking up in tufts.

"Manu can have it," said Jasmine. "I'll be back in a minute."

"Cool," said Manu, plonking himself on a chair.

Mom looked astonished. "But you always fight for the first pancake."

Jasmine left the room to avoid having to reply. Manu was already reaching for the syrup.

Toffee was lurking outside her bedroom door again. Jasmine tutted at him.

"I'm never going to let you in while the birds are there," she said as she picked him up and opened the door. "So you might as well give up trying." And she set him down on the landing and shut the door behind him.

Peanut and Popcorn were cheeping again, their necks at full stretch and their beaks gaping.

"Bird parents must be exhausted the whole time, with a nest full of chicks to feed," Jasmine said to them, dropping food into their mouths. "And they have to find the food themselves. I only have to open a packet."

Suddenly she remembered that she wasn't

supposed to talk to the chicks. She closed her mouth tightly. It was so hard not to speak to baby animals.

When she went back to the kitchen, Manu was kneeling by the Aga, stroking the little lamb. "He's so cute," he said to Jasmine. "I'm going to call him Derek."

"He's already got a name," said Jasmine. "He's called Lucky."

"Derek's a better name," said Manu. "Can I make cupcakes today, Mom?"

"I'm not sure I've got the strength," said Mom as she slid a pancake onto a plate for Jasmine. "It took about a week to clean the kitchen after you made cupcakes last time."

"There's still some icing on the ceiling," said Jasmine, squeezing lemon juice on her pancake.

"That was Ben," said Manu. "He was doing a gravity experiment."

"Yes, well, it might be nice if Ben didn't do

quite so many of his experiments in our kitchen," said Mom.

A tremendous sound came from the Aga. Jasmine looked across the table.

Lucky was scrambling for a foothold. He scrabbled around frantically with his little hooves. Then, with what looked like an enormous effort, he heaved his front legs upright.

"Oh, good boy," said Jasmine. "Well done, Lucky. See if you can stand on your back legs, too."

Lucky scrambled and pushed and arched his back, and then finally he half climbed, half fell out of the Aga, and there he was, standing on the tiled floor on his own four legs. Jasmine jumped up from the table, knelt down, and kissed his head.

"Look at you, Lucky! You're standing up all by yourself."

The back door opened.

"Dad!" called Jasmine. "Come and look at this."

Dad appeared in the kitchen doorway, still in his coat and boots. He smiled and shook his head ruefully as he looked at Jasmine and Lucky.

"I should have known it was a bad idea to let you check the sheep. The minute I turn my back you bring another animal into the house."

"That's very rude," said Jasmine. "You should be thanking me. I just saved his life. Well, me and Mom."

She told Dad the whole story as she ate her pancakes.

"Well done, Jas," he said. "I knew I could rely on you to do the right thing. It's a shame about that ewe, though. She had a lovely pair of twins last year, no problems at all, and she seemed perfectly healthy yesterday."

"I'll do a postmortem later," said Mom. "There might have been some internal bleeding."

Just then, Lucky took two shaky steps on his gangly front legs.

"Look," said Jasmine. "He's walking."

Lucky took another couple of steps on his front legs. Jasmine frowned.

"He's not moving his back legs. They're just dragging along the floor."

Mom watched Lucky as he took a few more

wobbly steps with his front legs. His back legs dragged behind him.

"There must be something wrong with them," said Mom. "If he's not walking properly in a couple of hours, you might have to teach him to move them, Jasmine."

"Maybe he just likes walking like that," said Manu. "If I had four legs, I wouldn't just plod along. I'd move all my legs in different directions."

"How should I teach him?" asked Jasmine.

"Try pedaling his back legs gently in cycles while he's standing on his front legs. That should help get them moving properly. And you can bounce him gently up and down on his back legs as well, to strengthen them."

"I'll do it," said Manu. "I'll teach him some tricks, too."

"You will not," said Jasmine, glaring at him. "You're not touching any of my animals ever again."

After an unfortunate incident at Christmas with a litter of kittens, Manu had been banned from handling any of Jasmine's animals without permission.

"That guy in Foxdean said there'd been another case of sheep rustling," Dad said as he poured syrup over a pancake.

"Near here?" asked Manu.

"No, down in Cornwall this time. Poor devil woke up to find half his flock gone."

Ella appeared in the doorway, a book in her hand. "Ooh, pancakes," she said. "Are there any more lemons?"

"In the fridge," said Mom.

Ella was about to open the fridge when she spotted Lucky.

"What a cute lamb! He's so tiny!"

"He's mine," said Jasmine proudly. "He's called Lucky."

Mom and Dad looked at each other. "Just to

be clear, Jasmine," said Dad, "you realize he'll be going back out to the barn tomorrow, as soon as he's had all his colostrum?"

"But he'll still be mine," said Jasmine. "I'll still be feeding him."

"We'll foster him with another ewe," said Dad. "Much cheaper and less labor-intensive than bottle-feeding."

Jasmine stared at her father, outraged.

"I just saved his life," she said, "and you're telling me I can't keep him?"

"You wouldn't be able to keep him forever anyway," said Dad.

Jasmine knew only too well what Dad meant by that remark. Ewe lambs were kept in the flock for breeding, but ram lambs were sold at the market when they were old enough.

"He'll have to go out in the field with the flock in the long run," said Dad, "so it would be better to find him a foster mother."

"You can't send him out to the barn tomorrow," said Jasmine. "He can't even walk properly. And what if another ewe doesn't want him?"

"Well, we'll try to find one who does," said Dad. "And you can still spend time with him and do his leg exercises."

"But I want to keep him. I'll look after him better than a ewe would."

"Jasmine, you promised you wouldn't pester us for any more animals, remember?" said Mom. "You've got quite enough to look after, especially now with Sky's sheepdog training."

Well, thought Jasmine, *that settles one thing anyway.* She definitely wasn't going to tell Mom about the birds in her wardrobe.

"But it's Easter vacation," she said. "I've got plenty of time. And when I go back to school, he won't need feeding so often."

"He'd still need at least three feedings a day," said Dad, "and you know I don't have the time

to bottle-feed lambs while you're at school."

Jasmine opened her mouth to argue, but Dad jumped in first. "You heard what Mom said. No pestering. We'll match that lamb up with a foster mother tomorrow."

7

A Rat on the Loose

Jasmine phoned Tom after breakfast. He arrived in time to watch Mom give Lucky his second dose of colostrum.

"I've been thinking," Mom said as she withdrew the stomach tube. "I've got the afternoon off on Monday. I could take you both to the swimming pool in Maybury. You know, the one with the wave machine and the water slides."

Jasmine's eyes lit up. "Oh, yes! I've been wanting to go there ever since it opened."

But then she saw Tom looking at her, and she trailed off. Of course they couldn't go swimming when Peanut and Popcorn had to be fed every half hour.

"What about Lucky?" she said, stroking the tiny lamb snuggled in her lap. He was so warm now that he felt like a little hot water bottle. "We can't leave him on his own."

"He'll be with a foster mother by then."

"But he might not be strong enough."

"Well, let's wait and see, shall we? If he still needs looking after, we could leave it until next weekend."

"Yes, maybe," said Jasmine. But she knew they wouldn't be able to go next weekend, either. The chicks would still need feeding every forty-five minutes.

Mom looked at her questioningly. "You've been asking me to take you to that pool for ages, and now you sound as though you don't want to go at all."

"I do," said Jasmine. "I really do. I just think we should wait and see how Lucky's doing."

"You're behaving very oddly at the moment, Jasmine," said Mom.

A piercing scream came from upstairs, followed by the sound of running footsteps.

"A rat!" cried Ella, bursting into the kitchen. "There's a rat upstairs! Do something! I'm leaving! I can't stay in this house while there's a rat on the loose."

Manu and Ben rushed in from the mudroom, where they had been making a potion from dead leaves and shower gel. They were grinning with excitement.

"We'll catch it," said Manu. He ran back into the mudroom and reappeared with a baseball bat, which he handed to Ben, and a cricket bat for himself. "Where is it?" he asked eagerly.

"In Jasmine's room," said Ella. She shuddered. "I heard it squeaking. It was *so* horrible."

Manu and Ben rushed out of the room, waving their weapons above their heads.

"I think it was in the wardrobe," Ella called after them.

Tom and Jasmine shot each other horrified looks.

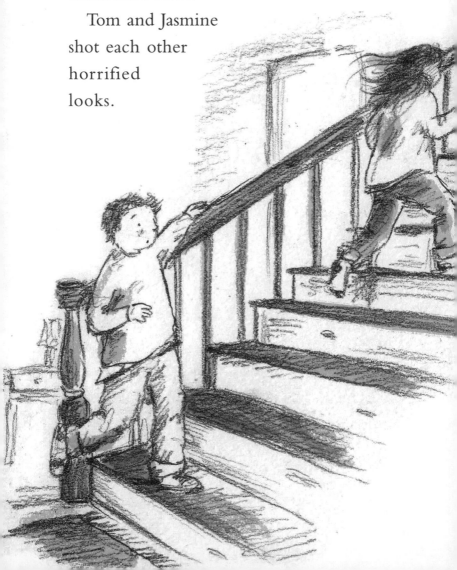

Then Jasmine handed Lucky to Mom and they sprinted from the room.

"Manu, stop!" yelled Jasmine. "Don't go in my room! Stop!"

"Kill the rat! Kill the rat! Kill the rat!" chanted Manu and Ben as they stomped up the stairs.

Jasmine and Tom raced after them, bursting into Jasmine's room just as Manu, brandishing the cricket bat, yanked the wardrobe door open.

Jasmine leaped across the room and tugged the bat out of Manu's hand. Tom grabbed the baseball bat from Ben.

Manu rounded furiously on Jasmine. "Hey! What are you doing? We're trying to catch a rat!"

"We'll do that," said Jasmine, shutting the wardrobe and spreading her arms in front of the doors. "Get out of my room, you two."

61

"No," said Manu. "We want to see the rat."

"It will have run away by now anyway," said Tom.

"No, it hasn't," said Ben. "I can hear it squeaking."

Manu listened. He frowned. "That doesn't sound like a rat."

"It's not a rat," said Jasmine.

"What is it, then?"

Jasmine thought quickly. "It's my cheeping bird toy. I must have left the sound on."

Manu looked at her suspiciously. Then he looked across to her bookcase.

"There's your bird toy."

"Oh," said Jasmine.

Seeing her confusion, Ben and Manu ducked under her arms and, before she could stop them, they pulled the wardrobe doors open. There were the baby birds, their necks stretched high and their beaks gaping open as they cheeped frantically in their nest.

"Whoa, what are they?" asked Ben.

"They're so cool," said Manu.

Jasmine glanced at Tom in despair just as Dad and Mom appeared in the doorway.

"So, did you catch the terrifying rodent?" Dad asked.

"There isn't a rodent," said Jasmine flatly.

"I'm not surprised. With the racket those boys made, I should think every rat within a fifty-mile radius has gone into hiding."

"It's baby pterodactyls," said Manu. "Look."

Dad raised his eyebrows. "If Jasmine's been breeding dinosaurs in her wardrobe, we definitely need to take a look."

Jasmine looked at Tom, defeated. He shrugged. The game was well and truly up.

She lifted the nest out of the wardrobe.

"They're baby birds," she said. "They're called

Popcorn and Peanut. We found them on the barn floor yesterday, when we were checking the sheep."

Mom and Dad came closer to get a better look.

"Did you keep them in the wardrobe all night?" asked Mom.

"Yes."

"Why didn't you tell us?"

"You were TB testing."

"Not in the evening. You could have told us then." Her eyes widened. "So *that's* why you didn't want to go out for pizza. And why you didn't want to go to the swimming pool."

"We knew you'd make us take them to a rehabilitator," said Jasmine. "We wanted to prove we could look after them ourselves."

"How did you know what to do?" asked Dad.

"We looked it up online," said Tom. "There was tons of stuff."

"We did everything they said," said Jasmine.

"And they look healthy, don't they? They're just hungry. That's why they're cheeping."

"I'll get their food," said Tom, looking relieved to have an excuse to leave the room.

"Please don't take them away, Mom," said Jasmine. "Tom and I can look after them just as well as a rehabilitator could. And it would be so amazing to see them grow."

"I thought you didn't like birds in cages," said Mom.

"I don't. We want to release them into the wild when they're ready. Please, Mom? Please, Dad? It would be such good experience for when we have our rescue center."

Mom and Dad looked at each other. "Well," said Mom, "I'm impressed you've kept them alive, to be honest. Orphaned birds this young don't often survive."

Tom came back with the food.

"Can I feed them?" asked Manu.

"No," said Jasmine. "You have to do it right or they can choke. You can watch Tom feed them."

Tom took the nest over to Jasmine's bed. Ben and Manu followed him.

"So," said Jasmine to her parents, "can we keep them? Please say yes."

"What do you think?" Mom asked Dad.

"It's all right by me if it's OK with you," he said.

Mom smiled. "Well, you've both shown a lot of commitment, I have to say. I can't believe you turned down pizza and a swimming trip. And by the looks of it, you're doing a great job. So you can keep the birds until they're old enough to be released, if you promise that you will release them."

"Oh, thank you!" said Jasmine. "Thank you so much."

Tom beamed in delight. "Thank you so much."

Jasmine sensed an opportunity. "Since we're going to release the birds," she said, "can I keep Lucky, instead of giving him to a foster mother?"

Dad smiled. "Good try. But no."

"I'm already going to be doing his leg exercises," said Jasmine. "It would hardly take any more time to feed him. And Tom's going to come up every day, so there'll be two of us."

"If you're going to run a rescue center," said Dad, "you'll be releasing the animals or finding new homes for them when they're ready, won't you? So I'm afraid you're just going to have to get used to letting them go."

8
That Should Fool the Ewe

"That's right, Lucky," said Tom as he bounced the lamb's back legs gently up and down. "You're definitely getting stronger."

It was Sunday afternoon, and Tom was doing Lucky's exercises in the kitchen while Jasmine prepared his first bottle of formula milk. Mom had given him all his colostrum from the tube, and now Dad had asked Jasmine to give him a bottle.

"He needs to know how to suck before we

put him with a foster mother," Dad had said. "But we don't want to get him used to the bottle, or it might be harder to foster him."

Jasmine hoped it would be impossible to foster Lucky, and not only for her own sake. The most successful fostering usually happened when a lamb was matched with a ewe whose lamb had just died, and Jasmine certainly didn't want that to happen.

However, another method that sometimes worked was to trick the mother of a single lamb into thinking she had had twins. Sheep use their sense of smell to identify their own lambs, so you could rub the birth fluids on an orphan lamb and hope the ewe would think it was hers. Sometimes this worked and sometimes it didn't. If the ewe discovered the lamb wasn't hers, she might reject it violently. Jasmine dreaded this happening to Lucky, who was so small and defenseless. What if his back legs got even more damaged?

"I think that's enough exercise for now," said

Tom. "I don't want to tire him out. Should we try him with the bottle?"

Jasmine settled Lucky on her lap, tucking his long skinny legs underneath his tiny body. She stroked his soft ears. They had fluffy edges that showed how woolly he was.

Tom handed her the bottle. She prized Lucky's mouth open and slipped the teat in. Lucky jerked his head away and the teat slipped out.

"Come on, Lucky," said Jasmine. "You need to learn to suck."

She pulled his jaws apart and positioned the teat in his mouth. Lucky jerked his head away again.

"How about if I hold his head?" said Tom. So this time, when Jasmine slipped the teat into Lucky's mouth, Tom gently held his head in place. But Lucky still didn't suck.

"Try moving his jaw up and down," said Jasmine, "to teach him what to do."

Tom did so. After a few seconds, Lucky wiggled his tail.

70

"He must be tasting the milk," said Jasmine. "He likes it."

Slurpy sucking noises came from the lamb. Slowly, Tom moved his hands away from Lucky's head, until he was just gently cupping his chin. Lucky sucked the milk noisily and vigorously.

"That's great," said Jasmine, a big smile on her face. "Well done, Lucky."

When Lucky had finished, Jasmine set him on the floor. He stood unsteadily on his wobbly legs

and gave a high-pitched bleat. Then he shook himself and wiggled his tail.

"Let's see if he can walk better," said Tom. He went to the other side of the kitchen and crouched down. Jasmine joined him.

"Lucky!" called Tom. "Come here, Lucky!"

Lucky gave another little bleat. Then, with his front legs, he took a couple of tottering steps. His back legs still dragged along the ground.

"I guess it will take a bit longer," said Jasmine. "At least he's drinking, though."

Tom glanced at the clock. "Time to feed Popcorn and Peanut."

The back door rattled open and Dad appeared in the kitchen doorway.

"Ah, good, you're here. There's a ewe out there that just had a single lamb. Bring this one out and we'll put him with her."

Jasmine hugged Lucky to her. "Do we have to? I don't think he's strong enough. What if she hurts him?"

"Come on, Jasmine. You know it's easier and cheaper to put him with a ewe. And it will be better for him in the long run. He's got to go out with the other sheep at some point, so he might as well go now."

Jasmine gave a big sigh. Silently, she stood Lucky on the floor while she tugged on her boots and shrugged her arms into her coat.

"I'll go and feed Popcorn and Peanut," said Tom.

Jasmine blinked back the tears that were pricking at the corners of her eyes. "Thanks, Tom," she said. Then she picked Lucky up, followed Dad out the back door, and trudged across the farmyard.

In the barn, Dad had put the new mother and her lamb in a small pen on their own. He took the new lamb out of the pen. Then he took Lucky and rubbed his head, tail, and back end against the newborn lamb's wet coat.

"That should fool the ewe into thinking he's hers," he said.

 73

He put the ewe's own lamb back in the pen, next to the mother. She turned and sniffed his head as he began to suck from her udder.

"OK," said Dad softly. "Now put the other one in."

Full of sadness, Jasmine lowered Lucky into the pen. The ewe turned her head and sniffed him. Then, with a movement so swift that it took Dad and Jasmine completely by surprise, she lowered her broad head and butted him away. Lucky flew across the pen and landed in the straw, sprawled out and winded.

"You see!" cried Jasmine as she gathered him up. "You can't do this. She hates him."

"It can take a while," said Dad. "They don't usually accept a new lamb right away."

Jasmine laid her cheek against Lucky's face. "You poor little thing. Are you all right?"

Lucky bleated and nibbled her ear.

"She'll get used to him," said Dad. "We'll tie her up so she can't headbutt him."

He fetched a rope halter from the corner of the barn and climbed into the pen.

"Hold her head steady," he said.

Burning with resentment, Jasmine held the ewe's big woolly head as Dad attached the halter and tied the rope around the rail.

"Put him back in there, Jas."

Jasmine glared at her father's back. Then she kissed Lucky's head and lowered him into the pen. She held her breath as he dragged himself over to the ewe. The sheep tugged at her collar and swung her head to and fro to try to free herself. When that didn't work, she aimed a swift kick at Lucky.

The little lamb went flying. He crashed into the metal rail with a force that made Jasmine cry out in horror.

"He's bleeding!"

She scooped him out of the pen. There was a gash on his left back leg, just above the knee, where the ewe's sharp hoof had struck him.

Dad frowned and shook his head. "They don't usually kick," he said.

"You can't put him back in there," said Jasmine, holding Lucky tightly to her. "I won't let you. I'm not letting him go until you promise I can look after him."

"She might accept him eventually," said Dad, "if he were big and strong enough to keep trying. But she's clearly going to put up a fight, and he's not going to be able to take much more of that."

"He's not going back in there," Jasmine repeated. "I'm going to look after him myself."

Dad gave a rueful smile. "All right, Jasmine. You win."

Jasmine gave a cry of delight. "Oh, thank you, Dad! Did you hear that, Lucky? I'm going to be your foster mother, not that nasty old ewe."

"Bed up that empty pen," said Dad. "Put plenty of straw down, and I'll stack a couple of those small bales around it, to keep out drafts."

"I'll ask Mom to treat that cut on his leg, too," said Jasmine.

"He ought to go under a heat lamp really," said Dad, "but I'm reluctant to use one again, after last year."

Jasmine shuddered at the memory. Last spring, the lambing barn had caught fire when a heat lamp fell on the floor and set the straw alight.

"No, don't use a heat lamp," she said. "I've got a better idea. I'm going to make him a thermal jacket."

Dad raised his eyebrows. "Really? I didn't think you liked sewing."

"There's no sewing. Just packing tape and Bubble Wrap."

"Bubble Wrap?"

"Mom said at the clinic they make little blankets out of Bubble Wrap for hamsters and guinea pigs when they're recovering from operations, to keep their body heat in. So I'm going to make Lucky a Bubble Wrap jacket to keep him warm."

Dad nodded thoughtfully. "Well, it's definitely worth a try. If it works, you can patent it and make your fortune."

"I'll do that," said Jasmine. "Then I can use the money for my animal rescue center."

She should be completely happy now, she thought as she walked back to the house. She had a lamb and two baby birds to look after. But there was a little dark cloud at the edge of her happiness. She tried her best to ignore it, but it kept pushing its way back in.

In just a few weeks' time, she would have to say goodbye to all of them.

9
Will She Be OK?

Peanut and Popcorn grew rapidly. At five days old, their shiny round black eyes opened and they started to look at each other.

"They're imprinting on each other," said Jasmine. "That's really good. They know they're birds now."

The next day, they began to crawl around the nest and flap their little wings. By the time they were eight days old, they had the beginnings of tiny brown and black feathers.

"I think they're sparrows," said Jasmine, and when she asked Mom to come and look, Mom told her she was right.

That week, the nestlings stood upright on their skinny legs for the first time. By eleven days, their feathers were soft and fluffy.

"I wish we could stroke them," said Jasmine longingly.

"You're going to have to resist," said Mom. "You've done really well, you know. They've imprinted on each other, not on you, and that's exactly how it should be."

The nestlings didn't need food coloring to tell them apart anymore. Peanut had the pale brown back of a female sparrow, whereas Popcorn had a black bib at his throat and a male sparrow's reddish-brown back.

When the birds were twelve days old, Jasmine found them hopping around at the bottom of her wardrobe. It was time to put them in a birdcage so they could learn to fly. Mom borrowed a cage

from her office and Dad hung it in the lambing barn. Young sparrows had to learn their songs from other sparrows, and there were always sparrows in and around the barn.

When the spring quarter began again, Jasmine brought the birdcage into the mudroom every day after school and let Peanut and Popcorn out so they could practice flying for longer distances. At first, they stayed mainly on the floor, just taking a few tentative short flights. But every day they flew higher and farther. When they were tired or hungry, they just flew back into the cage.

Although Jasmine still hand-fed them a few times a day, they began to eat more of their food from a bowl. They also started to peck at the bird seed she scattered on the cage floor.

One Saturday morning, they didn't open their beaks when Jasmine approached with the tweezers. She waved her hand above their heads to create a shadow, to imitate the shadow the parents

made when they arrived at the nest with food. But the sparrows ignored her.

"You don't want me to feed you anymore, do you?" she said to them sadly, withdrawing her hand. "You're fully weaned."

Peanut hopped to the open cage door, flapped her wings, and flew up to the work surface. Jasmine dropped a few seeds on the surface nearby, and Peanut pecked them up.

CRASH!

The noise came from Manu's room, directly above the mudroom, as something very heavy fell to the floor. Peanut flapped her wings in panic, flew across the mudroom at full speed, and smashed right into the window. Jasmine cried out in terror as the bird's little body slid down the glass. It landed on the work surface and lay there, silent and unmoving.

For a few terrible seconds, Jasmine stood rooted to the spot, her heart pounding. Then she dashed through the kitchen and into the hall.

"Mom!" she shouted. "Mom, come here!"

"What is it?" called Mom from upstairs.

"Peanut's injured. Badly. Come, quickly."

But as Jasmine ran back into the mudroom, an even more terrible sight met her eyes. On the work surface stood Toffee, with Peanut clamped between his jaws.

Jasmine's heart stopped. She sprang across the room. "No!" she shouted. "No! Put her down!"

Toffee sprang to the floor, with Peanut still in his mouth, and ran toward the kitchen. Jasmine lunged for him, but he was too quick for her.

"Toffee, put her down!" shouted Jasmine. She ran after him into the kitchen just as Mom opened the other door. Toffee changed direction,

and Jasmine grabbed him by the scruff of his neck. Startled, he dropped Peanut.

"Bad cat!" said Jasmine. "Bad, bad cat!"

She took him out to the garden and shut the door behind him. She locked the cat flap and ran back into the kitchen.

Mom and Jasmine stood over the little bird. Peanut lay on her side, her eyes closed, motionless except for the rapid beating of her heart.

Jasmine dreaded what Mom might say, but she had to know.

"Will she be OK?" she whispered.

"She doesn't have any visible injuries," said

Mom. "Hopefully, she's just stunned. We'll wait and see."

Jasmine held her breath. They waited for what seemed like a very long time. Then Peanut opened her eyes. Jasmine gave a gasp of relief.

Peanut closed her eyes. Jasmine's stomach lurched. She watched the little bird fearfully.

Peanut opened her eyes again. She jerked her body, flapped her wings, and staggered to her feet.

"Oh," whispered Jasmine.

Mom was smiling. "She's recovering from the concussion."

Peanut stood quietly for several minutes, opening and shutting her eyes, while Mom and Jasmine watched. Then she turned her head and looked at them. She turned her head the other way, as if refamiliarizing herself with her surroundings.

"Do you think she's all right?" asked Jasmine.

"I think she'll be fine," said Mom. "She seems to be recovering well. What happened to her?"

Jasmine told her. "It was all Manu's fault," she finished. "Dropping things like that."

Mom raised her eyebrows and looked at Jasmine. "You know what this means, though, don't you?"

"What?" said Jasmine.

"If she's flying strongly enough that she can knock herself out by flying into a window, then they're ready to be released."

"But I already have to take Lucky out to the field this morning."

"Remember what you promised?" said Mom. "You need to set them free."

"I will," said Jasmine. "I want to set them free. But I can't let them all go in one day. I'll release the birds tomorrow. I promise."

10
Lots of Space to Play In

When Tom arrived an hour later to help take Lucky and the other lambs to the field, Peanut was chirping happily in her cage again. Jasmine told Tom the whole terrible story as she put her boots and coat on and they walked across the yard.

All the lambs started to bleat as Tom and Jasmine approached the barn. Lucky's bleat was the loudest of all. He scampered to the gate to greet Jasmine, running with his front legs and jumping with his back ones. He could pick up his back legs now, but, despite all the pedaling exercises, he couldn't move them separately. He was much stronger, though, and no longer needed his Bubble Wrap jacket.

Jasmine picked him up and he nibbled at her ear. She laughed and turned her head away. "That tickles! Stop sucking, Lucky. It's not time for your feeding yet."

Lucky started nibbling at a loose strand of her hair. Jasmine pulled his jaws apart with her fingers and extracted her hair from his mouth. His little teeth were quite sharp now.

She set the lamb down. He bleated again and began to suck at the hem of her pants.

"You're going to live in a field now, Lucky," she said. "You're going to taste grass for the first time. And Sky and I will walk up to feed you every day before and after school."

It was a beautiful day. The sky arched high and blue over the farm, and the blackthorn bushes frothed with white blossom. The pussy willows

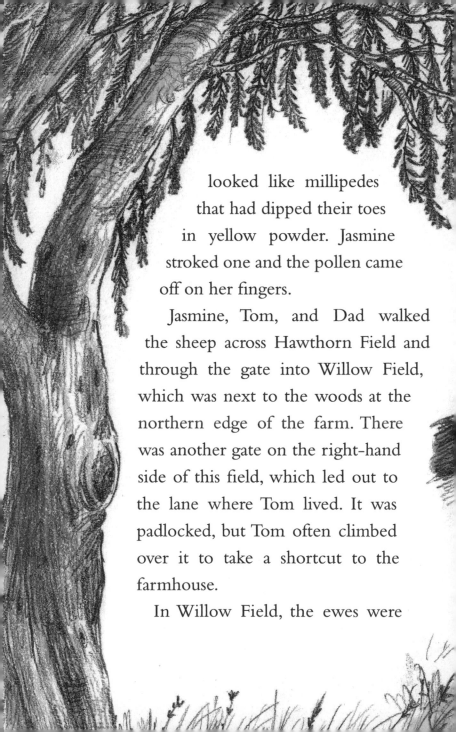

looked like millipedes that had dipped their toes in yellow powder. Jasmine stroked one and the pollen came off on her fingers.

Jasmine, Tom, and Dad walked the sheep across Hawthorn Field and through the gate into Willow Field, which was next to the woods at the northern edge of the farm. There was another gate on the right-hand side of this field, which led out to the lane where Tom lived. It was padlocked, but Tom often climbed over it to take a shortcut to the farmhouse.

In Willow Field, the ewes were

grazing peacefully or sitting down chewing cud.
Some of the lambs were feeding. Others sat
nestled into their mothers' woolly fleeces. One
group of more adventurous lambs was racing
around the field in a gang, running, skipping,
and doing funny little sideways jumps.

"Look, Lucky," said Jasmine. "Lots of space to
play in and friends to play with."

Lucky bent his head down and took an experimental nibble of grass. He clearly liked it, because he immediately started pulling up more.

"Lovely sight, isn't it," said Dad, "seeing all the ewes with their new lambs out here for the first time. It always makes me think back to those first four ewes I bought thirty years ago."

As a teenager, Dad had saved up money from his work on the farm and bought four pedigree Southdown ewe lambs to start his flock. Most of the sheep in this field were descended from those four lambs.

Dad set off around the edge of the field to check the sheep.

"The other lambs are all so much bigger than Lucky," said Jasmine. "I hope they won't bully him. Do you think he'll be all right?"

"It's a shame Betty isn't in this field," said Tom. "She could have looked after him."

Betty was a lamb that Jasmine had bottle-fed the previous year. She was still very tame, and ran

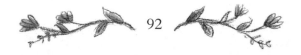

over to greet Jasmine every time she came to her field. Last year's lambs were in a different field, though, so Betty wouldn't be able to look after Lucky.

"Where is Lucky anyway?" asked Tom.

Jasmine glanced down, but Lucky was gone. She scanned the sheep nearby, but she couldn't see him.

Suddenly, Tom laughed. "Look," he said, pointing to a fallen tree trunk in the middle of the field. A gaggle of lambs was chasing one another around it, jumping onto the fallen tree and off again. And right in the middle of them was Lucky, half running, half jumping, and clearly having a wonderful time.

Jasmine watched him, her feelings a mixture of pride and sadness. Tom glanced at her.

"He's still yours, you know," he said. "You told me that sheep remember their human friends even after years apart. Lucky will always come when you call him, like Betty still does."

"I know," said Jasmine. "But he'll only be here for a few more months."

"Do you think your dad might let you keep him?"

"No," said Jasmine. "He's not a good enough specimen to be a breeding ram, and I'm not allowed any more pets. So . . ."

She couldn't bear to finish the sentence, but they both knew how it would end. In a few months' time, Lucky would be sent to market.

11
Headlights

In the middle of the night, Jasmine was woken by terrible screams outside her window. She sat up in bed, her heart pounding. What was going on?

Then she realized what it was. A fox fight.

She got out of bed, opened her curtains, and looked down over the moonlit garden. She couldn't see any foxes.

She looked out across the fields. Then she frowned. There were headlights shining at the edge of Willow Field. Headlights belonging to a big vehicle, by the look of it.

Why would there be a vehicle in the sheep field at this time of night? Was it Dad's truck? Had something happened with the sheep? But it looked too big to be Dad's truck.

Jasmine ran out of her room, along the landing, and into her parents' room.

"Dad? Mom?"

"Jasmine?" It was Mom's sleepy voice.

"Is Dad there?"

"Yes, of course. Why?"

"There's a vehicle up in the sheep field. I thought it was his truck."

Mom switched on her bedside lamp. "A vehicle?"

"What's going on?" Dad mumbled.

Mom was wide awake now. "Jasmine saw a vehicle in the sheep field."

"What?" Dad jumped out of bed and grabbed his jeans from the chair.

"What are you doing?" asked Mom.

"Going up there, of course."

Jasmine opened the curtains. "Oh. It's gone."

Dad looked out the window. Then he turned to Jasmine. "Are you sure you saw a vehicle?"

"Yes!" said Jasmine indignantly. "There were big headlights."

"But was it definitely in the sheep field?" asked Mom. "Could it have just been in the lane? The driver might have stopped to make a phone call or something."

Jasmine began to doubt herself. "I'm sure it was in the field. But maybe it wasn't."

Dad looked at her for a few seconds. Then he said, "Well, it won't do any harm to drive up there and check. Better safe than sorry."

"Take your phone with you," said Mom. "Call me if you need me."

Jasmine followed Dad out of the room and down the stairs. In the hall, she said, "I'm coming with you."

"Don't be silly, Jas. It's two in the morning. Go back to bed."

"I won't be able to sleep until I know the

sheep are safe. I'll go back to bed as soon as we get home, I promise."

"But you're not even dressed."

"I'll put my coat and boots on over my pajamas."

"Oh, all right, then. But hurry up. I need to go."

Sky jumped up from his bed as Jasmine came into the mudroom for her boots.

"Do you want to come with me?" she said, taking his leash from the hook on the back of the door. "We might need a sheepdog."

She thought Dad might make a fuss about Sky coming, but he didn't even seem to notice. Sky sat quietly at Jasmine's feet on the passenger side as they drove up the farm driveway and along the lane. Dad drove fast and looked tense. He didn't say a word.

As the gate to Willow Field came into view, Jasmine cried out in dismay. It was wide open.

Dad swore under his breath and swung the truck through the gate. They both jumped out. Frantically, Jasmine scanned the field, desperately

hoping to see the flock huddled together in a corner. But the field was empty. Every single sheep was gone.

She looked around for Dad. He was standing at the gate, as still as a statue, staring at the padlock. She walked over to him.

"They've sawn through the chain," he said. His voice was so quiet and flat that she could hardly hear the words. "They've taken the whole flock."

"Call the police," said Jasmine. "Where's your phone?"

As if in a daze, Dad pulled his phone out of his pocket. Then he put his hand on the gate to steady himself. He looked blankly at the phone screen.

"What's the number?" he said.

"Give me the phone," said Jasmine, holding out her hand. "I'll call the police."

12
I'm Not Going Home

"Why are they taking so long?" Jasmine said for the umpteenth time.

Dad said nothing. He hadn't said a single word since Jasmine had taken his phone to call the police. He hadn't even been able to call Mom and let her know what was happening. Jasmine had texted her instead. Dad was just staring into the empty field. He seemed to be frozen with shock.

Where were the police? It was so frustrating that Jasmine thought she might explode. The poor sheep had been bundled into a truck and carted off to who knew where, and she and Dad were just standing in an empty field, waiting.

She couldn't get the image out of her head of poor little Lucky and all the other ewes and lambs, crammed into a truck by a gang of criminals and hurtled around the countryside, thrown against the sides of the vehicle as it sped around corners, their poor hooves skidding around on the metal floor.

What if they were injured? They might break their legs. It was all too horrible to think about, yet she couldn't seem to stop.

She paced back and forth. Vehicles went by on the main road in the distance, but not a single one came up the lane.

Eventually she saw headlights turn off the main road, and a police car approached, driving very fast.

"Finally," she said, turning to Dad. "They're here."

 102

Dad shook his head as though he was waking up from a trance. The car stopped in the gate and he walked stiffly over it.

Two police officers got out, a man and a woman. They introduced themselves as Officer Lambert and Officer Blake, and then they started asking Dad questions. He answered slowly, and Jasmine had to prompt him on some of the answers. The woman wrote things down on a clipboard. They asked a lot of details that seemed completely irrelevant to Jasmine. Why weren't they just trying to catch the thieves and rescue the sheep?

When Dad told them that it was Jasmine who had seen the truck, they questioned her, too. Then they walked away a few paces and held a muttered conversation. Officer Lambert went back to the police car and made a phone call. Officer Blake walked over to Jasmine and Dad. She looked very serious.

"Obviously we don't know yet who stole your

sheep," she said, "but one possibility is that they might have taken them to an illegal slaughter-house."

Dad clutched the gatepost. Jasmine stared at her in blank horror. An illegal slaughterhouse?

"We've had our suspicions for a while about a place over in Liston," Officer Blake said. "We suspect that, as well as their legal operations, they've been accepting stolen animals and selling the meat illegally. We don't have enough evidence for an arrest yet, but this is the largest group of animals to have been taken in this area, and we're not too far from Liston. It's a distinct possibility that that's where they're headed."

Dad found his voice. "Well, what are you waiting for? Let's go after them."

"That's exactly what we're going to do," said Officer Blake.

"My partner is calling for backup and another car will meet us there."

"Good," said Dad. "Let's get going, then." He strode to his truck and opened the driver's door.

Officer Blake held up her palm. "My colleagues and I will handle this," she said. "We'll keep you updated as soon as there's anything to report."

Dad laughed in disbelief. "You tell me my sheep are about to be slaughtered by a bunch of criminals and then you tell me to go back home

to bed? I'm sorry, Officer Blake, but I'm heading straight over to that slaughterhouse. Come on, Jasmine."

"Mr. Green, if this is a criminal group, they could be highly dangerous. You and your daughter need to go straight home and not hinder the investigation. We'll keep you fully informed."

She walked over to the car and opened the passenger door.

"But if you do find sheep there," said Jasmine, "how will you know if they're ours?"

"If we find any sheep," said Officer Blake, "we'll call you to come and identify them."

"But Liston's at least an hour's drive away," said Dad. "A fat load of good it will be if you call us in an hour's time and it takes us an hour to drive to Liston and then the sheep you've found aren't ours. Our sheep could be a hundred miles away by then."

And they could be dead, thought Jasmine.

"I'm sorry," said Officer Blake, "but this could

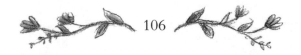

106

be an extremely dangerous operation and it needs to be handled by trained police officers. I must ask you to go home and not obstruct police business. We'll be in touch as soon as we have anything to report."

She got into the passenger seat and shut the door. Officer Lambert backed the car out the gate. The engine noise faded into the distance and the lane was silent again.

Jasmine turned to her father. "Come on, Dad. Let's go."

"I'm not going home," said Dad. "Not while my sheep are being driven around the country-side by criminals."

"I wasn't talking about going home," said Jasmine. "The police can't stop you from driving around in your own truck, can they? So let's go find our sheep."

13
Organized and Ruthless

It was only after they had been driving for half an hour that a question occurred to Jasmine.

"Do you actually know where you're going, Dad? They didn't say where in Liston the place was."

"There's a farm on the outskirts," said Dad, "with a couple of industrial units. There have been rumors for a while that there's something fishy going on there. I'm pretty sure that's the place they're talking about."

After what seemed like hours, he pulled over on a grass embankment just outside a gate that led to a farm driveway.

"Is this it?" asked Jasmine.

"Yes." He turned off the engine.

Jasmine frowned. "Why are you stopping? Why aren't we going up the road?"

Dad gave her a serious look. "Listen, Jas, the police were right about one thing. People who steal an entire flock of sheep like that in the middle of the night—they're not going to be nice people, and it's not going to be the first time they've done this. They'll be organized and ruthless. So we're going to let the police handle them. As soon as they phone and say they've found the sheep, we can be in that farmyard in two minutes, instead of the hour it would take if we had to set off from home. That's why we're here, OK?"

Jasmine sighed. "OK."

But she couldn't stop worrying. What if their

sheep weren't here at all? What if they were on their way to an illegal slaughterhouse in a completely different place? What if she never saw Lucky again?

Jasmine felt sick.

"Can I open the window, Dad? I need some air."

Dad turned the engine on so she could put down the window. She leaned out and took a deep breath.

"Ugh. Look at that litter. Disgusting."

Someone had thrown a whole load of trash into the hedge. There were drink cans, chip bags, and sandwich wrappings lying on the ground.

"How can people do that?" she said. "Why don't they just put it in a trash can?"

Then she spotted something among the litter. A small piece of yellow plastic. Her stomach churned. An ear tag.

She opened the door and scrambled out of the truck. From the direction of the farmyard came distant sounds of shouting, banging, and

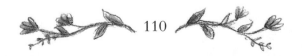

clattering. Suddenly she was worried about the police officers. What if the sheep rustlers were armed?

"Jasmine?" said Dad. "What are you doing? Get back in. Now."

Jasmine picked up the piece of plastic and got back in. She held it out to Dad. His eyes widened and he snatched it from her. He turned on the light above his seat and looked at the numbers on the tag. Then he swore under his breath. Jasmine felt the contents of her stomach turn to water. She didn't need to ask him whether the tag belonged to one of their sheep.

"That's what they did in Yorkshire, isn't it?" she said. "It said so in *Farmers Weekly*. They took off all the ear tags and threw them away, to stop the sheep from being identified."

"Well, I don't know what the police are playing at," said Dad, "but I'm not staying here while my sheep are being slaughtered at the end of that road." He reached for the ignition.

"Wait a second," said Jasmine. "I bet the other tags are here, too."

She jumped out of the cab and began to rummage in the trash. Sky leaped out, too, and started lapping water from the ditch that ran under the hedge.

"Get back in," called Dad. "Let's go up there. That tag will be enough to prove they're ours."

Jasmine was about to get back in when she caught a glimpse of something orange in a patch of stinging nettles. She reached into the nettles, feeling the stings prick her hands and wrists.

She pulled out a plastic shopping bag. The handles were tied in a double knot. Jasmine ripped a hole in the bag.

It was full of ear tags.

She took one out and handed it through the window to Dad. He read the number.

"That's ours," he said. "Let's go."

Suddenly, Sky started to bark.

"Shh, Sky," said Jasmine, stuffing the bag into her coat pocket. "Be quiet."

Sky continued to bark. He was standing in the gate, looking up the farm driveway.

"What is it?" she asked. She walked over to see what he was barking at. It was a long road, and she couldn't even see the farmyard.

Then she froze.

In the dim moonlight, she could just make out the silhouette of a man running down the road toward them.

"Dad," she whispered. "Someone's coming."

Dad leaped out of the truck and sprinted to the gate. "Get in the truck!" he hissed.

But Jasmine stayed rooted to the spot. Sky was barking frantically now. The man glanced around, as if looking for a gap in the hedge.

Dad raced toward him. Sky bounded after Dad, and Jasmine followed them. The man turned and started sprinting back toward the farmyard. Sky

ran in front of him, and he tripped and fell. He swore and cried out in pain.

Something fell out of his pocket.

A gun.

He reached out to grab it, but Dad dropped to his knees and pinned the man to the ground.

"Don't touch that gun," he said to Jasmine, in a

calm, steady voice. "Now get my phone from the truck and call the police."

Jasmine ran over to the truck, her heart beating very fast. She'd never seen a handgun before, and it was terrifying to be so close to a live weapon.

The man swore at Dad and tried to get up, but Dad kept him firmly pinned to the ground, face-down on the rough road. Sky stood in front of his face, baring his teeth and growling.

Jasmine called the police as she hurried back to Dad. The man was kicking out, but his legs just kicked the air. He tried to free his arms again, but Dad kept hold of them. Sky stayed in position, growling softly.

Suddenly, Jasmine had an idea. She ran to the truck and took out a length of baler twine. Then she ran back to Dad.

"We can tie his wrists together behind his back," she said. "Like handcuffs."

"Get off me," snarled the man, "or I'll sue you for assault."

"Really?" said Dad. "Will that be before or after you go to jail?"

And then, around the corner from the direction of the farmyard, appeared a police car. It braked just in front of them and three officers jumped out. Officer Blake held a pair of handcuffs. Two of them took an arm each and handcuffed the man's arms behind his back. Officer Blake started telling him he was under arrest.

"Enough about him," said Dad. "Just tell me what's happening to my sheep."

14
He'll Come Running

"We caught the others in the farmyard," Officer Blake told Dad and Jasmine, once the other two officers had retrieved the gun and taken the man off to the police station, "but this one managed to get away. Thank you for stopping him, I suppose. Although we really wish you'd stayed at home."

"It was Sky, honestly," said Jasmine. "He tripped him. Can he have a medal?"

The police officer laughed, which Jasmine found rather insulting.

"We raided the slaughterhouse," said Officer Blake, "and arrested several men who were waiting to slaughter the sheep."

"Where are the sheep?" asked Dad. "Are they safe?"

"Safe and sound," said Officer Blake. "Only just, though. They'd been put in a holding yard. We got here in the nick of time."

Dad rested his hand heavily on Jasmine's shoulder. "Thank goodness you woke up and saw that truck, or we'd have lost them all. Let's get them home."

"Wait a second," said Officer Blake. "It's not quite as simple as that."

"What do you mean?"

"We've had a call from a man who says he farms over in Bellingham. He claims to have lost a flock of Southdown sheep tonight. He thinks these sheep are his."

Cold dread clutched at Jasmine's stomach. If the sheep on this farm weren't theirs, then

 118

where were their sheep? And what was happening to them?

"What do you mean?" said Dad. "What man in Bellingham?"

"I'm sorry, but I can't give you his name."

"I don't know anyone in Bellingham with a flock of Southdowns," said Dad. "Show us these sheep and I'll tell you whether they're mine."

"I'm afraid we can't just go on your word," said Officer Blake. "We're going to need proof before we can return them to you."

"We've got proof," said Jasmine. She reached into her pocket and pulled out the bag of ear tags. "We found these on the embankment. The thieves must have taken them off in the back of the truck and thrown them away. They're definitely from our sheep. Dad knows the numbers."

Officer Blake looked impressed. "Nice work," she said, taking the bag. "We can do all the checks to make sure these are your ear tags. But since the tags aren't actually on the sheep anymore, it

would help right now if you had another way of proving that the sheep are yours. Do you have any other means of identification?"

"I've got tons of photos," said Jasmine, "but my camera's at home."

Dad had been frowning in silent thought. Now he said, "I'm absolutely certain there's no one in Bellingham with a flock of Southdowns this size. That man who phoned you must be tied in with the criminals who took our sheep."

Jasmine's mouth fell open as she realized what he was saying. "Yes! When they got caught, one of them sent him a message, and then he phoned and pretended the sheep were his."

"That is a possibility, of course," said Officer Blake, "and we'll obviously check his claims, but this will all take time. Are you sure you don't have any other way of identifying the sheep?"

"Yes!" cried Jasmine, kicking herself for not having thought of this before. "If you take us to them, I can prove right now that those sheep are ours."

"Really?" said Officer Blake. "How's that?"

"My pet lamb is in that flock. He'll come running to me when I call him. And he has a very special way of running."

"Come on," said Dad. "Let's head up to the yard."

"I have to warn you, they're not being kept in very nice conditions," said Officer Blake.

"All the more important that we get them home quickly, then. Let's go."

They bumped up the road to the derelict farmyard bordered by tumbledown buildings. Dad parked the truck and they jumped out, landing in a squelch of dung and mud.

Officer Blake didn't need to tell them where the sheep were. They could hear the baas and bleats across the mucky yard.

As they drew closer, Jasmine began to make out the dim shapes of a huddled mass of sheep, crammed together in a filthy pen on the other side of the yard.

 121

"Lucky!" she called. "Lucky!"

The sheep let out a deafening din of baas and bleats. Jasmine called Lucky again, but he didn't appear. Maybe he was crammed in so tightly that he couldn't push his way through.

"Lucky!" she called. "Come here, Lucky!"

And then, through all the other sheep voices, she heard it. Lucky's high-pitched little bleat. She would have recognized it anywhere.

There he was, pushing, ducking, and weaving his way through the flock. He propelled himself through the bars and raced toward Jasmine, running on his front legs and jumping on his back legs. Jasmine crouched down in the stinking mess, gathered him into her arms, and hugged him tightly. Lucky bleated and sucked the collar of her coat.

Jasmine turned to Officer Blake with tears in her eyes.

"This is my lamb," she said. "This is Lucky."

15
A Very Lucky Lamb

By the time Jasmine finally got to bed, it was already light. She slept until the early afternoon. When she came downstairs, Manu bombarded her with questions about the police and the man with the gun.

"I wish I'd been there," he said. "I would have kicked all those men and knocked their guns out of their hands and then made sure they never had guns again."

The doorbell rang. "That'll be Tom," said Jasmine.

"You'd better let him in, then," said Mom. "I expect you've got a lot to talk about. Your father and I certainly do."

Once Tom had heard all the details and got over the shock (helped by several chocolate cookies), he and Jasmine went out to see the lambs. Tom had an old soccer ball tucked under his arm. "I thought the lambs might like it," he said.

Dad had put the sheep in the closest field to the farmyard, right next to the barn. "It's not the best grass," he'd said, "but I'd rather have them nearby at the moment."

Tom climbed over the fence and kicked the ball toward a group of lambs. One of the bolder ones galloped up and started dribbling it across the field with his head. The others ran, skipped, hopped, and jumped behind him, throwing their back legs into the air in joyful, wild leaps.

The leader stopped, and the other lambs gathered around the ball, sniffing it curiously. One of them nudged another with his head,

and they started to play fight. Then Lucky began to dribble the ball, and the others all set off in happy pursuit.

As Tom picked up the ball and kicked it back to the group of lambs, Jasmine's gaze wandered to the barn. It looked so empty now that lambing season was over. But Popcorn and Peanut were still there, cheeping in their cage. And on a straw bale facing them stood two wild sparrows, singing their hearts out to the fledglings.

The fledglings, Jasmine was sure, were answering them.

She took a deep breath.

"Tom?"

"What?" said Tom, running over to retrieve the ball.

"I think we should set the sparrows free."

Tom looked at her in surprise. "Right now? Are you sure?"

"They're ready. It wouldn't be fair to keep them any longer. Let's do it before I change my mind."

Standing in front of the cage, Jasmine took a last long look at her sparrows, trying to fix them in her mind so she would remember them forever. Then she opened the door.

"Goodbye, little birds," she whispered. "Have a lovely life."

Part of her hoped the sparrows wouldn't want to leave. But as soon as she stepped back from the cage, Peanut hopped to the door, spread her

127

wings, and flew out of the barn into the nearby bushes. Then Popcorn hopped up into the doorway, spread his wings, and followed her.

Tom glanced at Jasmine, but she didn't look back at him. She kept her eyes fixed on the bushes and said nothing. Tom watched with her for a while, but when the sparrows didn't reappear, he went back to the sheep field.

Jasmine sat on a bale, gazing into the thicket,

until she remembered she had to write a story for school the next morning.

She fetched her exercise book and brought Lucky to the barn to keep her company.

"What should I write about, Lucky?" she asked him.

A sparrow flew from the beams above her into one of the trees outside the barn. Jasmine looked up at the barn roof, remembering the day she had found Peanut and Popcorn.

An idea began to form in her mind. She picked up her pen and started to write.

The first thing I remember is falling. Falling out of my cozy nest. Falling a long, long way and landing in a rough tangle of straw.

The story came into her head so fast that her pen could barely keep up with her ideas. Jasmine

was so absorbed that, until Lucky tugged at her pant leg, she didn't notice the two little sparrows pecking in the straw at her feet.

"Popcorn?" she said. "Peanut?"

The sparrows' shiny black eyes looked into Jasmine's for a second. Then they beat their wings and flew away, disappearing into the branches of a hawthorn tree.

Jasmine stroked Lucky's soft, warm ears and turned back to her exercise book. Lucky nibbled her sleeve as she wrote the final words of her story.

The girl opened the door of my cage.
"Fly, little one, fly!" she whispered.
I was gone in a flutter, calling my final farewells.
For I am a bird, and birds fly free.

She sat in silence for a moment. When she looked up, she was surprised to see her parents walking toward the barn.

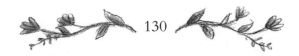 130

Mom glanced at the empty cage, and then at Jasmine.

"You've set them free?"

Jasmine's throat felt tight. She couldn't speak. She just nodded.

Mom hugged her. "You should be very proud of yourself, Jas. It's not easy to look after animals for so long and then let them go. You've done a really good job."

Jasmine pulled back from the hug. She wasn't in the mood. Any second now, they would start talking about how she would soon have to let Lucky go, too.

"Dad and I have been talking," said Mom. "We're so grateful to you for saving the sheep. If it weren't for you, we would have lost them all."

"We think you deserve a reward," said Dad. He smiled at her. "How would you like to keep Lucky?"

Jasmine stared at Dad and then at Mom, hardly able to take this in.

 131

"Really?" she said. "I can keep Lucky? Forever?"

"It seems only right," said Dad, "after what you did last night."

"Oh, thank you, Dad!" said Jasmine. "Thank you, Mom! Thank you so much!"

She knelt down in the straw and hugged the lamb. "Did you hear that, Lucky? You get to stay with me forever."

Lucky bleated and licked her ear.

"You named him well," said Mom. "He's certainly brought us luck."

"I knew he would," said Jasmine. "He's a very lucky lamb."

Acknowledgments

Thank you to my niece Rosie Hobbs, who allowed me to use extracts from her story "Epic" in the final chapter of this book. And thank you to Eden and Emily in the Scottish Borders, who suggested that I name the lamb Lucky.

Turn the page for
an interview with Jasmine and
a sneak peek of the next book in the
JASMINE GREEN RESCUES series!

A Q&A with Jasmine Green

What is your favorite part about lambing season?

There are so many great things about lambing season that it's hard to choose a favorite! I love going out to check the ewes in the morning and seeing the new lambs that were born during the night. I love getting to see a birth; it's always amazing how quickly newborn lambs are able to stand up and start feeding. I also love bottle-feeding and cuddling the orphaned lambs and the ones who need extra milk.

Are there differences between caring for birds and caring for mammals?

I think the main difference is that newborn mammals need colostrum, which is their mother's first milk. If they don't have it, they won't survive, so you have to give them a colostrum substitute if they haven't had it from their mother. Birds don't drink milk, so you have to make sure you give them the right food. Often, baby birds can be fed canned dog food in an emergency. Another difference is that some birds will attach themselves to the first animal they identify after hatching from the egg, and that might be a human! This is called imprinting, and if you want the bird to be able to survive in the wild, you can't let it imprint on you, which is sometimes quite tricky!

How do lambs make friends in the field?

It's so nice to watch lambs playing together. They have so much fun racing around, leaping about, and butting each other as they play. Sometimes a lamb will kick its back legs in the air to show another lamb that it wants to play. Sometimes it will walk up to another lamb and place its chin on the other lamb's back or neck as an invitation.

Lambs also play king of the castle, where they take turns standing on a rock or hill. When another lamb approaches, the lamb on the rock will defend its position by butting or pushing the other lamb away. Each lamb stays on the rock for a few minutes before giving the next lamb a turn!

How many animals do you have now?

I have Truffle the pig, who lives in the orchard and sleeps in a kennel with my dad's spaniel, Bramble. I also have Button the duck. I rescued him when he was just an egg, and now he lives in the farmyard with the chickens. My collie, Sky, sleeps downstairs in the farmhouse, and my two cats, Toffee and Marmite, sleep on my bed. And now I have Lucky the lamb, too! He lives in the field with the other sheep, but he always runs to greet me when I go out to see him.

Jasmine Green Rescues

Rescues

A Goat Called Willow

1
Kid For Sale

"You can buy yourselves a souvenir, or spend it on fairground rides and cotton candy, whichever you like," said Mom, handing some money to Jasmine and her best friend, Tom. "Meet me back here at four o'clock, OK?"

"Wow, thanks, Mom," said Jasmine, looking in delight at the money.

"Thank you very much, Dr. Singh," said Tom.

"Can me and Ben go off on our own, too?" asked Jasmine's little brother, Manu.

"Certainly not," said Mom. "You two need to stay with me."

"But that's not fair!"

"When you're ten, you can go off without me," said Mom. "Jasmine wasn't allowed to wander around the sheep fair on her own when she was six."

"Come on, Sky," said Jasmine, giving her sheepdog's leash a little shake. "Let's go and see the sheep."

The Fenton Sheep Fair was held every year in a big field on a farm in the South Downs. There was a fairground, a craft tent, and all sorts of stalls selling food and drinks. But, for Jasmine and Tom, the main attraction was the sheep.

They made their way to the top of the field. Here, several rows of pens had been built from metal rails, with walkways between the rows. Each pen contained a small group of sheep, all washed and groomed to perfection.

A voice crackled over the sound system. "The

next class to be judged will be Southdown ewe lambs. Could all entrants make their way to the show ring now, please."

"You should have entered Lucky," said Tom.

Lucky was Jasmine's pet lamb. His mother had died when he was born, and Jasmine had bottle-fed him until he was old enough to live on grass.

"I wanted to enter him," said Jasmine. "But Dad's too busy with the cows to come to the fair, and Mom was working this morning."

Jasmine's dad was a farmer and her mom was a farm vet, so they were always busy looking after animals or doing office work.

"Let's go and see the lambs in the ring," said Tom. "I bet none of them are as cute as Lucky."

They walked between the pens toward the show ring. In some of the pens, farmers were brushing their sheep's woolly coats. One woman was oiling her sheep's hooves to make them shine.

"Oh, look!" said Jasmine. She hurried along the walkway to get a closer look. "Oh, it's so cute!"

In the far corner of the farthest pen sat a beautiful baby goat. Its coat was mainly brown, with patches of black and white on its legs and back, and a white blaze down the middle of its face. As Jasmine and Tom leaned over the gate, the kid greeted them with a high-pitched bleat.

"Oh, you're so sweet," said Jasmine. "Come here so I can stroke you."

"It's a girl," said Tom. "Look, she's for sale."

He pointed to a handwritten notice tied to the bars of the pen.

FEMALE KID FOR SALE

Jasmine's eyes widened. "Oh, I wish we could buy her."

Tom laughed. "Imagine how mad your mom and dad would be if you did."

Jasmine already had six animals of her own, and her parents had told her that she wasn't allowed to have any more. She and Tom planned to run an animal rescue center when they grew up. So far, they had rescued a runt piglet, a motherless duckling, an abandoned puppy, a rejected kitten, two baby sparrows, and an orphaned lamb.

They had released the sparrows when they were fully grown, and Holly the kitten now belonged to Tom, but Jasmine had persuaded her parents to let her keep Truffle the pig, Button the duck, Lucky the lamb, and Sky the sheepdog. She also had two cats called Toffee and Marmite.

"Anyway," said Tom, noticing a price written in below the sign, "with the money your mom gave us, we could only buy half of her."

The little goat stood up, bleated, and took a few tentative steps toward the children. Jasmine stroked her back.

"Her coat's so soft," she said. "Feel it, Tom. Sorry, little goat. I can't buy you, but I hope you find a lovely home."

"Mind your backs," said a gruff voice behind them.

They turned to see a man leading two sheep on halters. The children stepped away from the gate so he could open it and take the sheep inside.

"Excuse me," said Jasmine in her politest voice. "Is this your kid?"

He grunted in a tone that Jasmine understood to mean yes.

"She's beautiful," said Jasmine. "How old is she?"

"Four weeks," he said, taking the halter off one of the ewes. "If you're not going to buy her, clear off. I've had enough time-wasters asking pointless questions."

"Actually, I'm thinking about buying her," she said, giving him a look that she hoped made it clear she was a serious farmer about to do a deal.

"Well, don't think about it much longer. I'm heading off shortly."

A flicker of hope rose inside Jasmine. If nobody

bought the goat today, maybe she could persuade her parents to let her buy it later.

"What will you do if you don't sell her today?" she asked.

"Shoot her."

"Shoot her!" Jasmine was so shocked that her words came out as a squeal. "No! Why would you do that?"

"The mother just died," he said, "and I don't have time to bottle-feed the kid. I was going to shoot her yesterday, but since I was coming here, I thought I might as well bring her and see if anyone fancied hand-rearing. Seems like nobody else has the time either, though. I'll shoot her as soon as I get back."

Jasmine was suddenly filled with determination. She had no idea how she was going to manage it, but she knew one thing. She wasn't going to allow this tiny animal to be shot.

"We'll buy her," she said.

Tom gave her a worried look.

"We don't have all the money with us now," Jasmine said, "but we can give you half and pay the rest later."

"Where do you live?" he asked.

"Oak Tree Farm. In Westcombe."

He looked at her with slightly more respect. "So you're Mike Green's girl."

Jasmine nodded.

"Is your dad here, then?"

"No, but my mom is."

"And they don't mind you buying a goat?"

"Of course not," said Jasmine, crossing her fingers. "They love goats. We can't take her home right now, though. We'll have to get everything ready. Would you be able to deliver her tomorrow?"

"Martin!" called somebody from the other side of the pen. "How are you? Haven't seen you for ages."

The two men started to chat. Tom grabbed Jasmine's sleeve.

"What are you doing?" he whispered.

"What?" said Jasmine innocently. "Mom said we could buy a souvenir. She never said it couldn't be alive."

"You know she won't let you buy her."

"She doesn't need to know," said Jasmine. "I've got enough money saved up."

"But what about—"

"Tom, do you want this beautiful little goat to be killed tonight?"

Tom sighed. "Of course I don't."

"So don't worry about anything else. We'll work it all out later. The only thing that matters right now is that we save her life."

Jasmine Green Rescues

A Piglet Called Truffle

Helen Peters
Illustrated by Ellie Snowdon

Jasmine Green Rescues

A Duckling Called Button

Helen Peters
Illustrated by Ellie Snowdon

WALKER BOOKS

Jasmine Green Rescues

A Lamb Called Lucky

Helen Peters
Illustrated by Ellie Snowdon

WALKER BOOKS

Jasmine Green Rescues

A Goat Called Willow

Helen Peters
Illustrated by Ellie Snowdon

WALKER BOOKS

Which animals have you helped Jasmine rescue?

- ☐ A **Piglet** Called **Truffle**
- ☐ A **Duckling** Called **Button**
- ☐ A **Collie** Called **Sky**
- ☐ A **Kitten** Called **Holly**
- ☐ A **Lamb** Called **Lucky**
- ☐ A **Goat** Called **Willow**

About the Creators

Helen Peters is the author of numerous books for young readers that feature heroic girls saving the day on farms. She grew up on an old-fashioned farm in England, surrounded by family, animals, and mud. Helen Peters lives in London.

Ellie Snowdon is a children's author–illustrator from a tiny village in South Wales. She received her MA in children's book illustration at Cambridge School of Art. Ellie Snowdon lives in Cambridge, England.

Truffle found
this way

Oak Tree Farm

Willow found
this way

← To village and school

Tom's
house